KJL010-1

DARKWING DUCK...CRIME-FIGHTER, BAD ELVIS IMPERSONATOR.

SUDDENLY! ST. CANARD IS PLUNGED INTO DARKNESS!

COOL BEANS! THE WHOLE CITY IS BLACKED OUT!

MY INFRA-PINK ULTRA SCAN SPECS SHOULD LOCATE THE PROBLEM IN A JIFFY.

AHA! MEGAVOLT, THE MOST DANGEROUS CRIMINAL EVER, IS SABOTAGING THE POWER COMPANY!

WARN HIGH VOL KEEP OU

POP!

MEANWHILE...

POLICE

ARE YOU *SURE* WE'RE SUPPOSED TO BE HERE? THIS IS THE *POLICE STATION!*

THAT'S WHAT THE *BOSS* WANTS! AND YOU KNOW THE BOSS, KINDA NOW, KINDA WOW!

I JUST HOPE WE DON'T RUN INTO A...

...*POLICEMAN!!!*

BUSHROOT!

SERVING THE PUBLIC GETTING YOU DOWN? TIRED OF STARING AT THOSE STATION HOUSE WALLS?

THEN ENGAGE IN LIFE-THREATENING COMBAT WITH *BUSHROOT* AND *THE LIQUIDATOR!*

SPLASH!

AT THAT MOMENT, BACK AT DARKWING TOWER:

I KNEW YOU COULD DO IT! WHAT FLAVOR?

THAT'S NOT FUNNY! MORGANA! FIX ME!

OH, DARKWING! I'M SO SORRY... *FOOF!*

HAH! I'M BACK! IT WILL TAKE MORE THAN TWO TREACHEROUS TRANSGRESSORS TO TAINT THE TRACK RECORD OF...

DARKWING YAK!

CALLING ALL CARS... HEELLLP! HELP HELP HELP HELP!

SOUNDS LIKE THE POLICE NEED HELP!

DO YOU WANT ME TO COME WITH YOU?

NO! er...uh... THIS TIME IT'S TOO DANGEROUS! heh-heh-heh. JUST FIX ME.

SOON:

RUN FOR YOUR LIFE! IT'S A DINOSAUR!!!

I WONDER WHAT HAPPENED TO THE *CUSTOMERS?* MAYBE *BURGERS* WOULD SELL BETTER.

OH, NO! IT'S—

STEGMUTT!

B R A M!

DID SOMETHING BRUSH AGAINST ME? OH, HI, DARKWING DUCK. WANT A HOT DOG? *PLEEEEZ??*

OH, WHAT THE HECK.

75 CENTS, PLEASE.

I *KNEW* THERE WAS A CATCH.

LET'S JUST HOPE CRIME TOOK A BREAK WHILE I STOPPED FOR A HOT DOG.

HEY, DARKWING! WAIT! YOU FORGOT SOMETHING!

I'M SORRY, DARKWING. ARE YOU *BUSY*?

OH, NO, NO, *NO!* I'M HERE WITH THE MOST DANGEROUS CRIMINALS EVER, PLAYING *"LET'S PRETEND!"*

OO-BOY! I *LOVE* LET'S PRETEND! WHAT DO WE PRETEND *NEXT?*

LET'S PRETEND YOU HAVE A *BRAIN!* I HAD EVERYTHING UNDER CONTROL UNTIL *YOU* CAME ALONG!

OH, WHY DO I HAVE TO BE SUCH A DISGUSTING, CLUMSY DINOSAUR? WHY ME?? WHY, *WHY, WHY?!*

BAM! BAM! BAM!

OOPS.

DID I HEAR SOME-ONE SAY "OOPS"?

SLAM!

SQUISH!

10

FRANKLY, DARKWING, I'M CONCERNED...

FOUR OF YOUR ARCH-ENEMIES HAVE JOINED FORCES... AN UNUSUAL PHENOMENON INDEED! WE HAVE TOP SECRET WEAPONS HERE AT SHUSH, AND IF THEY SHOULD FALL INTO THE WRONG HANDS...

LIKE THIS SVACO-650 *PIE GUN*. IT'S CAPABLE OF MASS DESTRUCTION... AND UNTOLD LEVELS OF HUMILIATION.

RELAX, J. GANDER...YOU'VE GOT THE ONE AND ONLY *DARK-WING DUCK* ON THE CASE!

GASP!

NEGADUCK! SO *YOU'RE* BEHIND ALL THIS!

BAH!

DARKWING AND LAUNCHPAD HEAD TOWARDS HOME.

FIRST THEY TOOK OUT THE POLICE STATION, THEN THEY TOOK OUT *SHUSH!* THIS IS *GREAT!* THE BIGGEST BATTLE OF MY CAREER!

THE FEARLESS FIVE AGAINST *ME!* ALL ALONE WITH NO HELP FROM *ANYONE!*

UH...YOU MEAN YOU AND--

--THE NATIONAL GUARD HAS BEEN CALLED IN TO HELP RESTORE ORDER TO THE NOW LAWLESS CITY OF ST. CANARD!

ACTION 9 NEWS

THE *NATIONAL GUARD???* WHAT COULD BE WORSE?!

AND LOOK! HERE COMES DUCKBURG'S HOMETOWN HERO...

...GIZMODUCK! NOW THE CITY IS SURE TO BE SAVED!

THE *LAST* THING I NEED IS SOMEBODY STEALING MY SPOTLIGHT!

AHHH, GEE, *DW.* THEY *DID* WIPE OUT THE POLICE AND *SHUSH* RIGHT UNDER YOUR *NOSE!*

ALL RIGHT, GIZMO! PACK UP YOUR BOY SCOUTS AND HIT THE BRICKS!

ME? HELP? HAH!!

MR. DARKWING! YOU NEVER GOT YOUR CHANGE!

DARKWING DUCK! HOW CONSIDERATE OF YOU TO OFFER YOUR ASSISTANCE!

SO, ARE YOU FOLKS HERE TO LEND A HAND, TOO?

STEGMUTT!

HI, GOSALYN!

NO NO NO NO!

NO ONE'S HERE LENDING ANYBODY A HAND! ALL OF YOU PEOPLE JUST GO HOME!!

UH, DW, THERE'S SOMETHING YOU OUGHTA SEE...

I'M PERFECTLY CAPABLE OF DEFENDING *MY* TOWN BY MYSELF, THANK YOU.

NOW!

CLICK!

HMMN

MMMM

BZZAAA AAPP!!

St. CANARD POWER & LIGHT

NOW THAT THERE'S NO ONE LEFT TO *STOP* US, LET'S TEAR UP THE TOWN!

SAYS *WHO?*

GASP!

SAYS THE *FEARSOME FIVE!!!*

HEY, YOU VILLAINS! DON'T MAKE ME COME UP THERE!

HERE, BOOBY! *CATCH!*

OH, BAD SHOW!

CRASH!

TIMELY INTERVENTION, DARKWING!

WHAT'S GOING ON UP HERE?

NEPTUNIA! NOT *HER*, TOO!

CRONCH!

ARE YOU HERE TO LEND A HAND, TOO?

THAT'S *IT!* YOU CAN BE A SUPER HERO *TEAM!* THE *JUSTICE DUCKS!*

I *LIKE* IT!

BUT WE'RE NOT DUCKS!

WE CAN BE *HONORARY* DUCKS!

WHAT DO *YOU* THINK, WINGEY?

SIZZLE!

POP!

CRACKLE!

THREE OF US CAN ATTACK FROM THE FRONT, WHILE THE OTHER TWO SUBVERSIVELY INFILTRATE...

I---

...DISGUISED AS *SINGING MONKS!*

THEN, AT THE APPOINTED HOUR... MORGANA, STEGMUTT AND I *LEAP* OUT OF THE *CAKE* AND...

ARRGH!!

OR... NOT!

NOT IS RIGHT! GO FIND YOUR *OWN* VILLAINS, 'CAUSE I CAN HANDLE THIS MYSELF, SEE?

EVERYBODY! JUST GO AWAY!!!

BZZZT!

AAAIIEEE

AND THAT'S THE *END* OF DARKWING DUCK!

AAAAAAA

I HOPE THIS IS ENOUGH MONEY!

OR *MEGAVOLT* WILL TURN OFF THE POWER TO THE *HOSPITAL!*

eh?

OKAY! *OKAY!* I'LL NEVER MOW THE LAWN AGAIN!

GRRRR ROWF ROWF!

HELP! THE *POLICE!!!*

WHAT HAVE I *DONE?* THE FEARSOME FIVE HAVE TAKEN OVER THE CITY! AND IT'S ALL MY FAULT, BECAUSE I WANTED THE GLORY!

SNAP! SNAP!

SNAP!

SNAP!

MEANWHILE...

THE FEARSOME FIVE TOOK OVER THE CITY IN JUST *FIVE MINUTES!*

A LOT OF HELP *DARKWING* WAS!

TAKE HEART, GANG! *WE'RE* THE ONES WHO CAN STOP THEM!

NOT *ME*, SWEETIE. I'VE GOT BUSINESS AT SEA TO TAKE CARE OF!

WHAT IF SOMETHING *HAPPENED* TO HIM?

4

BUSHROOT!

MORGANA!

OH, WHERE IS DARKWING WHEN I NEED HIM?

DARKWING DUCK? HAH! HE'S JUST A SMEAR ON THE PAVEMENT!

OKAY, BOYS! HELP YOUR DADDY!

TASTE THIS, YOU VILE VEGGIES!

NOW THEY'RE JUST HARMLESS DAISIES!

I'LL SHOW YOU HARMLESS!

STOP THAT!

heh-heh-heh!

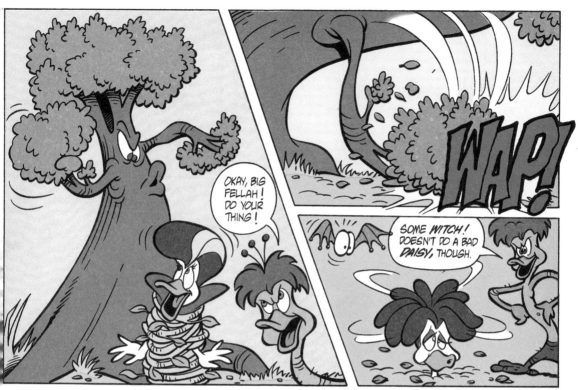

OKAY, BIG FELLAH! DO YOUR THING!

WAP!

SOME *WITCH!* DOESN'T DO A BAD *DAISY,* THOUGH.

MEANWHILE:

YOO-HOO, DARKWING! DARKWING *DUUUUCK!*

I GOTTA BE CAREFUL. *ANYBODY* COULD BE A VILLAIN. GOOD THING I'VE GOT A *DISGUISE!*

HOO HOO HAH HAH HAH!

SNAP!

ROBBED BY *TOYS!* HOW *EMBARRASSING!*

SNAP!

$

7

BACK AT DARKWING TOWER:

WHERE COULD THEY *BE?*

EW! A SPIDER!

WHAM!!

NO, LAUNCHPAD. IT'S MORGANA'S FRIEND *ARCHIE!*

WHAT *IS* IT, ARCHIE, OL' PAL? WHAT'S HAPPENED?

ECK ECK ZPTHTHT! WAAG! PLGAAH!

I COULD UNDERSTAND HIM IF HE DIDN'T *MUMBLE* LIKE THAT!

MORGANA'S BEEN *CAPTURED!* NOW THEY'VE GOT *ALL* OF THEM!

I'LL NEVER SEE MY *DAD* AGAIN, EVER! *BAWWWW!!!*

HELLO.

DAD! YOU'RE OKAY!

I'M *DIRT.*

I'M THE SELF-CENTERED BOOB WHO HANDS OVER THE CITY AT THE DROP OF A *DIME!*

BUT, DAD! THE TEAM *NEEDS* YOU!

THINK *SO?*

OF *COURSE* THEY DO! IT'S NOT TOO LATE! THE *JUSTICE DUCKS* AND I CAN STILL BE ONE! THE FEARSOME FIVE DON'T STAND A *CHANCE* AGAINST US!

?

SO...WHERE *IS* EVERYBODY?

15

AWWW. MY POOR ANVIL!

YESSSS! THE *PERFECT* DISGUISE!

NEGADUCK CAN'T TAKE ALL THE MONEY...

...WHILE *WE* DO ALL THE *WORK*...

IT'S *UNFAIR!*

'TIS *I*, MEN, YOUR *LORD* AND *MASTER*...

....NEGADUCK?!?

CREAM NEGADUCK! CREAM NEGADUCK!

BIFF!

SOK!

BOP!

CREAM *WHO???!!*

16

17

BAH! YOU'LL *NEVER* TAKE ME!!!

CHARGE!!!

DON'T *MOVE!!!* IF I PUSH THIS BUTTON, THE ELECTRONIC WALL WILL CLOSE AND *DESTROY* ST. CANARD!

:GASP!!!:

IN FACT...I THINK I'LL PUSH IT ANYWAY!

NO!!!!

oh, no.

22

A JOB WELL DONE, *JUSTICE DUCKS!*

SAY, YOU OLD CURMUDGEON! I THOUGHT YOU DIDN'T *WANT* A TEAM!

*Er... uh...*I DIDN'T SAY THAT...*OUT LOUD!*

NOW YOU CAN GO ON YOUR *DATE!*

WE'LL *ALL GO!*

OH, *NO,* YOU DON'T!

I CAN HANDLE *THIS* MYSELF!

C'MON, MORGANA. LET'S GET *DANGEROUS!*

End